WHO

took my shoe?

Written by Karen Emigh
Illustrated by Steve Dana

FUTURE HORIZONS INC.

Who Took My Shoe?
All marketing and publishing rights guaranteed to and reserved by

FUTURE HORIZONS INC.

721 W. Abram Street
Arlington, Texas 76013
800-489-0727
817-277-0727
817-277-2270 (fax)
E-mail: info@futurehorizons-autism.com
www.FutureHorizons-autism.com

Printed in Canada

Cataloging in Publications Data is available from the Library of Congress.

ISBN 1-885477-95-3

This book is dedicated to my son Brett, who was diagnosed with an Autistic Spectrum Disorder at the age of 6 years old. Because children with these disorders struggle to understand abstract language I wanted to write a book to help them better understand it. After just a year or so my son began to grasp the concepts of "who", "what", "where", "when", "why", and "how" by using the method in this book. I hope it can help your child too, as well as having a little fun along the way. Hopefully, one day researchers will find a cause and cure for Autistic Spectrum Disorders but until then parents, teachers, aides, etc. must do whatever we can to help our children reach their potential.

—Karen

Hi! I'm Brett.
I have lost my shoe.
My dog Herman and I will
now investigate. To find
my shoe, we will
search and ask
many questions.
Let's go!

took my shoe?

Did my brother Bryce take it? No.

Did a monster take it? No.

Did the mailman take it? No.

Then, who took my shoe?

happened to my shoe?

Did I leave it at school? No.

Did the wind blow it away? No.

Did Mom put it in the washing machine? No.

Then, what happened to my shoe?

is my shoe?

Is it under my bed? No.

Is it at the park? No.

Is it in outer space? No.

Then, where is my shoe?

did I lose my shoe?

When I went to recess? No.

When I went to swimming lessons? No.

When I went to Grandma's house? No.

So, when did I lose my shoe?

did I lose my shoe?

Because a magician cast a magic spell on it? No.

Because I wanted to? No, that's silly.

Because it's **L**ose **Y**our **S**hoe **D**ay?
No. That's REALLY silly.

Then, why did I lose my shoe?

can I find my shoe?

Should I dig for it in the back yard? No.

Should I do a "find your shoe dance"? No.

Should I call the police?
No. It's not an emergency.

Then, how will I find my shoe?

13

Wait just a minute... Herman **WHO** are you the one took my shoe?

Uh oh!

14

Herman...

is in your mouth?

Herman...

is my shoe?

Herman...

WHEN

did you take my shoe?

I'll just sneak out before he sees me.

Herman...

WHY

did you take my shoe?

How

did I find my shoe?

I used my brain and asked "who," "what," "where," "when," "why" and "how."

A NOTE TO PARENTS

Repetitive queues (whether they be physical, visual, etc.) help concepts fix themselves in a child's rote memory. Here are some examples you can practice with your child in everyday life.

Picking up the mail:
Who brings us the mail?
1) Does the fireman bring the mail? No.
2) Does the doctor bring the mail? No.
3) Does the mailman bring the mail? Yes! The mailman is who brings the mail.

A trip to the grocery store:
Where do we buy our food?
1) Do we buy it at the dentist? No.
2) Do we buy it at the pet store? No.
3) Do we buy it at the grocery store? Yes! That's where we buy our food!

You can do this in any situation.
When do you brush your teeth?
How do you brush your teeth?
Why do you brush you teeth?

Use your imagination and be silly. Kids love that! Try it and you'll find this can be a fun game for everyone and your child will not know you're teaching him/her important concepts. Good luck and best wishes.

– Karen

ABOUT THE AUTHOR

Karen Emigh is married to husband, Ken, and the mother of two boys Brett and Bryce. Karen began writing children's books as a way to help Brett, who is diagnosed with an autistic spectrum disorder, better understand abstract language. They reside in Northern California.

Illustrator Steve Dana is married to wife, Jodie, and is the father of Eric and Kelsey. They live in the same town as Karen Emigh.

More Great Books You'll Want to Read
from Future Horizons' wide selection on autism & Asperger's syndrome

Special People, Special Ways
by Arlene Maguire and Illustrated by Sheila Bailey

A beautiful picture book that encourages the youngest readers to think positively about people with disabilities. Written in easy-to-understand rhyming verses, this book suggests that everyone has something to contribute.

— only $14.95

Tobin Learns To Make Friends
by Diane Murrell

This colorful picture book teaches social skills as it tells how Tobin, a train, learns to make friends and engage in proper "train" social activities. Great book to "read aloud." For ages 3-8.

— only $16.95

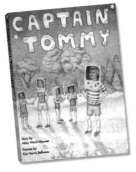

Captain Tommy
by Abby Ward Messner and Illustrated by Kim Harris Belliveau

This charming book has received wide recognition. For children, grades 1-4, it illustrates how one young boy, reluctantly at first, but with increasing interest, becomes an important contributor to the life of a fellow student with autism. Popular with "normal" students.

— only $14.95

My Friend with Autism
by Beverly Bishop and Illustrated by Craig Bishop

It's a fun coloring book that helps to encourage tolerance, education, and a positive approach to classroom integration for special needs children. This book was written so other students can better understand autism. A must for any classroom!

— only $9.95
(quantity discount available)

To order these or any of our wide variety of resources on autism and Asperger's Syndrome, call us at:

800-489-0727

or log onto our website at: www.FutureHorizons-autism.com
Feel free to call us with your questions or comments

JE/EMI

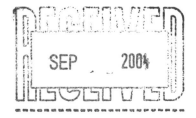